W9-CGS-491

# Prairies

Ted O'Hare

FITZGERALD BOOKS

Bethany, Missouri

Photo Credits:
Cover © Photodisc; Title Page © Tyler Olson; Pages 5, 9 © Millsrymer; Page 6 © Brian Erickson; Page 7 ©
Karachakov Evgeny Michaylovich; Page 8 © Darlene Tompkins; Page 11 © Frank Leung; Page 12 © Andrea;
Page 13 © Nicolas Nadjar, Danny Warren; Page 14 © James M Phelps, Jr; Page 15 © Midwest Wilderness;
Page 16 © Matt Ellis; Page 17 © Valerie Crafter; Page 19 © Len Tillim; Page 20 © Tyler Olson; page 21 ©
Duncan Walker; Page 22 © Michaela Steininger, Stephan Hoerold

Cataloging-in-Publication Data

O'Hare, Ted, 1961-
    Prairies / Ted O'Hare. — 1st ed.
    p. cm. — (Exploring habitats)

    Includes bibliographical references and index.
    Summary: Describes prairies—the grasslands of North
America and Canada, with very brief information on grasslands
in other areas of the world.
    ISBN-13: 978-1-4242-1384-9 (lib. bdg. : alk. paper)
    ISBN-10: 1-4242-1384-3 (lib. bdg. : alk. paper)
    ISBN-13: 978-1-4242-1474-7 (pbk. : alk. paper)
    ISBN-10: 1-4242-1474-2 (pbk. : alk. paper)

    1. Prairies—Juvenile literature. 2. Prairie ecology—
Juvenile literature. [1. Prairies. 2. Prairie ecology.
3. Prairie plants. 4. Prairie animals. 5. Grasslands.
6. Ecology.] I. O'Hare, Ted, 1961- II. Title. III. Series.
    QH541.5.P7O43 2007
    577.4'4—dc22

First edition
© 2007 Fitzgerald Books
802 N. 41st Street, P.O. Box 505
Bethany, MO 64424, U.S.A.
Printed in China
Library of Congress Control Number: 2006941000

# Table of Contents

The Land                                    4

Grasslands                                  6

Prairie Plants                             10

Prairie Animals                            14

Prairie Weather                            20

Prairies Tomorrow                          22

Glossary                                   23

Index                                      24

# The Land

In North America, grasslands are known as **prairies**. They are large expanses of fairly flat land, called plains. Prairies are located in the western part of the United States and Canada.

# Grasslands

Grasslands are generally treeless plains covered with grass. In some parts of the world this land is known by different names. In Argentina it is called **pampa**. And in **Eurasia** the land is called the **steppe**.

These grasslands are homes to many different plants and animals. The land is flat and does not have many trees. This is because the deep roots of prairie plants helped keep trees from taking root.

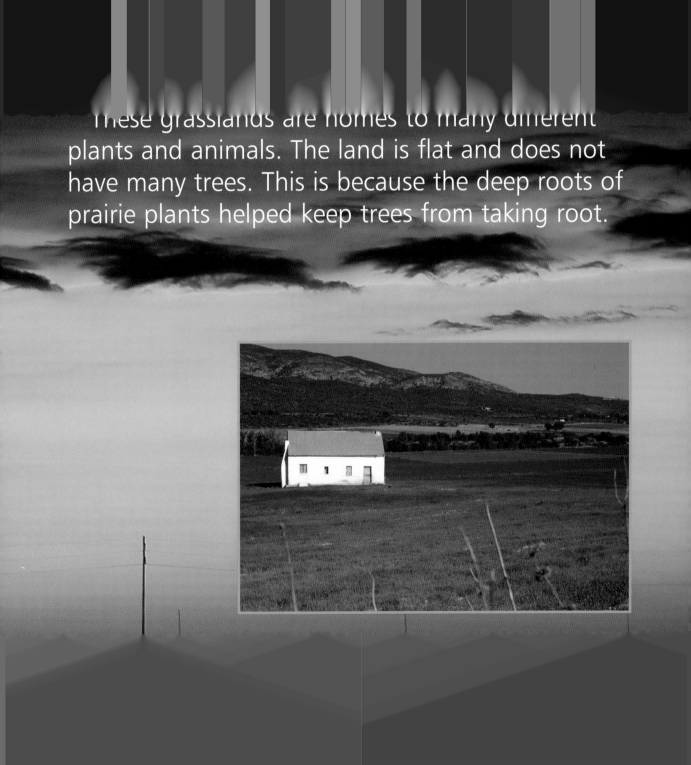

# Prairie Plants

Grassland plants are food for prairie animals. Coyotes prowl through the low prairie grass.

  Grassland plants provide shelter for animals. Some tall grasses protect prairie plants from strong sun and winds.

# Prairie Animals

Many prairie animals are runners. These include pronghorn antelope and deer.

15

Other animals like to dig. Diggers include the prairie dog and badgers.

The best-known prairie animal is probably the American bison, also known as the buffalo. There were once millions of them, but today there are only a few thousand.

# Prairie Weather

Prairie winters are harsh and windy. Most birds **migrate** south each autumn to avoid the snow and wind.

Summers are often hot and dry.

# Prairies Tomorrow

Prairies were once used primarily for **grazing**. More recently, farming has become an important way of life there.

# Glossary

**Eurasia** (YOUR ay zha) — land that is in both Europe and Asia

**grazing** (GRAYZ ing) — farm animals eating grass

**migrate** (MY grayt) — to make a journey from cold weather to warm

**pampa** (PAMP uh) — the name given to grasslands in Argentina

**prairies** (PRAIR eez) — the name given to grasslands in North America and Canada

**steppe** (STEP) — the name given to grasslands in Eurasia

# Index

bison  18
farming  22
grasslands  4, 6, 9, 10, 12, 23
grazing  22, 23

pampa  6, 23
plains  4, 6
steppe  6, 23

## FURTHER READING

Cole/Leeson. *Wild American Habitats: Prairies*. Blackbirch Press, 2003.

Howard, Fran. *Grasslands.* Buddy Books, 2006.

Jackson, Kay. *Explore the Grasslands.* Fact Finders, 2006.

Toupin, Laurie. *Life in the Temperate Grasslands*. Watts, 2005.

## WEBSITES TO VISIT

Because Internet links change so often, Fitzgerald Books has developed an online list of websites related to the subject of this book. This site is updated regularly. Please use this link to access the list:  www.fitzgeraldbookslinks.com/eh/pra

## ABOUT THE AUTHOR

Ted O'Hare is an author and editor of children's nonfiction books. Ted has written over fifty children's books over the past decade. Ted has worked for many publishing houses including the Macmillan Children's Book Group.